I'M
IN THE ZOO,
TOO!

I'M
IN THE ZOO,
TOO!

Brent Ashabranner

Illustrated by Janet Stevens

COBBLEHILL BOOKS / Dutton • New York

For Katrina and Trinity
— B.A.

Library of Congress Cataloging-in-Publication Data
Ashabranner, Brent K., date
I'm in the zoo, too! / Brent Ashabranner ;
illustrated by Janet Stevens.
p.   cm.
Summary: Anxious to be part of the zoo instead of
just living on the grounds, Burl the squirrel decides
to talk to the animals and find out how to get in.
ISBN 0-525-65002-4
[1. Squirrels—Fiction. 2. Zoo animals—Fiction.
3. Zoos—Fiction.] I. Stevens, Janet, ill. II. Title.
PZ7.A796Im   1989
[E]—dc19   88-32662
CIP
AC

Published in the United States by E. P. Dutton,
New York, N.Y.
a division of Penguin Books USA Inc.
Published simultaneously in Canada by
Fitzhenry and Whiteside Limited, Toronto
Typography by Kathleen Westray
Printed in Hong Kong
First edition   10 9 8 7 6 5 4 3 2 1

B url was a squirrel. He lived with his mother and father and sisters and brothers in a tall maple tree on the zoo grounds.

Everyone in his family searched for food from morning until night. Everyone except Burl. Sometimes he looked for food, but most of the time he went around the zoo and watched the other animals.

Burl was a curious squirrel. He wondered why crowds of people came to stare at the fringe-eared oryx and the ring-tailed lemur and the lions and polar bears and giraffes.

And he wondered about something else. Why did the zoo keepers bring food to those animals every day?

They brought fruit to the monkeys,

meat to the tigers,

hay to the zebras,

grain to the geese.

One night at supper Burl asked, "Why don't the zoo keepers bring us food like they do the other animals?"

His mother smiled and said, "They don't bring us food because we're not in the zoo."

"But we are in the zoo," Burl said. "Our tree is right in the middle of the zoo."

Then Burl's father said, "We do *live* in the zoo, but we're not *in* the zoo. There's a difference."

But Burl couldn't see any difference. The next day he set out to find out why he *lived* in the zoo but wasn't *in* the zoo.

He went first to Peacock's cage, climbed the fence, and jumped down beside the big bird. Burl would have helped himself to some breakfast grain, but Peacock was terribly stingy. He had whacked Burl on the head more than once for getting too near the feeder. So Burl stayed close to the fence and said, "What do you have to do to be in the zoo?"

Peacock shook himself and made a great fan out of his blue, green, and gold tail feathers. "You must have a beautiful tail," he said.

Burl turned his head and looked at his tail. It was bushy and stood straight up. "I have a beautiful tail," he said.

Peacock made a screeching noise that hurt Burl's ears. "Your tail isn't blue and green and gold," he said. "Beautiful tails have to be blue and green and gold."

Burl wasn't sure about that, so he went to the panda's enclosure. Panda was lying on her back, nibbling a piece of bamboo that she held between her front paws.

"I want to be in the zoo," Burl said. "What do I have to do?"

"You have to be cute," Panda said. "That's the main thing."

Burl wondered how anyone who weighed three hundred pounds could be cute, but he liked Panda and didn't want to hurt her feelings.

"I can wiggle my nose and ears at the same time," he said.

"I think that's a good start," Panda said, "but I don't know if it's enough to be in the zoo."

Then Burl went to where the gorilla lived and found the big black-furred beast lying under a tree looking up at the sky. Burl liked Gorilla because he was really a shy and gentle fellow despite his fierce look.

Burl sat down beside him and asked his question. "What do you have to do to be in the zoo?"

Gorilla sighed. "You have to frighten people," he said. "I'll show you."

He stood up and pounded his chest so hard the sound was like a drum.

Then he gave a great roar and ran down the hill toward a crowd of people who were watching him. The people screamed and jumped back.

Gorilla turned and looked back at Burl. "You see what I mean?"

Burl did see, but he didn't think he was quite big enough to frighten people that way. He decided to go on to the lion's den.

He found the big male lion sunning himself while people took his picture. Burl wasn't afraid because he knew Lion was as lazy as he was big. So Burl hopped up to him and asked, "What do you have to do to be in the zoo?"

"You have to be big and handsome so people will want to take your picture," Lion said.

Burl saw that people had their cameras pointed in his direction. "They're taking my picture," he said.

"They're not taking your picture," Lion said impatiently. "They're taking my picture. You're just in the way."

Burl knew Lion was right, but he didn't like the idea that he wasn't beautiful enough or cute enough or fierce enough or big enough to be in the zoo.

"If I had my own cage, people would take my picture," Burl said.

That gave Burl an idea. He had seen an empty cage where the gibbons and Colobus monkeys live, and he went there as fast as he could. The monkey cage was still empty, and the door was open. Burl hopped inside and jumped on a swing in the middle of the cage.

"I'm in the zoo, too!" he called out at the top of his voice.

A big Colobus monkey in the next cage looked at Burl. "You're just a squirrel," he said.

"I am an Eastern Gray Squirrel," Burl said with great dignity.

He did tricks on the swing. He raced up and down the wire screen. He jumped across the cage at a single leap.

Some people stopped to look at Burl. They laughed and
someone said, "Look at the squirrel in the monkey cage."
Two people took his picture, and Burl was very pleased.

Late in the afternoon a zoo keeper came around with food. Burl was glad to see him because he was very hungry.

The zoo keeper put food in each of the cages that had monkeys in them, but all he did when he came to Burl's cage was slam the door shut.

Burl jumped from the swing and looked in the food tray. It w̶ He couldn't believe that the zoo keeper had not

Burl looked over at the Colobus monkey who was munching a carrot. "The man didn't leave me any food," he said.

"Too bad," Monkey said. He finished the carrot and picked up a banana. "Maybe tomorrow."

"I can't wait until tomorrow," Burl said. "I'm leaving."

He went to the cage door and found that he could not open it. "How can I get out?" he asked Monkey.

"You can't get out," Monkey said.

"But how do *you* get out when you want out?" Burl asked.

"I can't get out," Monkey said crossly.

"You have to stay in that cage all the time?" Burl asked.

"Of course, I do," Monkey said. "And so do Lion and Panda and all the other animals in the zoo. And now, so do you."

Monkey was right. Burl couldn't find any way out of the cage. When darkness came, all the visitors left the zoo, and Burl felt lonely in the cage by himself. He thought about his mother and father and brothers and sisters. He wondered what they were having for supper. Burl knew they would be worried about him.

He got hungrier and hungrier. He hopped over to look in the food tray again, but it was still empty. At last Burl curled up in a corner and tried to sleep. He kept hearing strange noises, but finally his eyes closed.

He didn't wake up until he felt the sun warming his fur.
Burl was surprised that he had slept so long. He jumped
up, and the first thing he saw was a zoo keeper staring in
at him.

"What are you doing in there?" the man asked.

He opened the cage door and stepped inside. Burl shot between the zoo keeper's legs and out the open door. He ran home to his maple tree so fast his feet hardly touched the ground.

Burl's father and mother were waiting. They were very
happy to see him, but his mother said sternly, "Where have
you been, Burl?"

"I've been *in* the zoo," Burl told her.

"And how did you get *in* the zoo?" his father asked.

Burl started to tell him, but explaining was too hard. "Well,
I just did," he said, "but I've decided I would rather *live* in the
zoo than be *in* the zoo."

Then Burl went into their nest and ate some peanuts his mother had saved for him. His full stomach made him feel much better, and he began to think about yesterday.

It had been fun doing tricks and posing for pictures. He wouldn't want to do it every day, and he didn't want to be locked in a cage ever again.

But maybe he could visit Panda and Gorilla sometimes. He could do tricks on their trees and pose for pictures with them.

That would be fun. And he could be home in time for supper.